GRAND
EXERCISE

Songs and rhymes for energetic grandparenting

Compiled by Sheena Roberts
Illustrated by Rachel Fuller
Performed by Playsongs People

Stephen Chadwick, James Fagan, Kevin Graal, Stev[...]
Sandra Kerr, Nancy Kerr, Giles Leaman, Janet Russe[...] Leon
Rosselson, Debbie Sanders, Kaye Umansky, Rick Wilson, Tom Wright

PLAYSONGS PUBLICATIONS

For Linda

First published in Great Britain by Playsongs Publications Limited.
playsongs.co.uk

© 2021 Playsongs Publications Ltd

ISBN:
978-0-9517112-6-2

Printed in the UK by Ashley House Printing Company.
Sustainability: printed using green energy on FSC and carbon balanced paper and card, using vegan-friendly vegetable inks and non-plastic bio-gloss cover finish. Fully compostable, biodegradable and recyclable.

Text © 2021 Sheena Roberts. Illustrations © 2021 Rachel Fuller. Graphic design by Jocelyn Lucas. Sound engineering by 3D Music, and Powered Flight. Post production by 3D Music.

GRAND THANKYOUS

Many people have given their energy, their ideas, and their creativity to the making of this *Grand Playsongs* series. Particular thanks are due to Kaye Umansky, without whom I would never have started, and to Stephen Chadwick, without whom I would never have finished. Also to:

~ everyone in **Playsongs People** for their musical creativity, their fun-filled performances, their voices and their many other instrumental skills: Stephen Chadwick, James Fagan, Kevin Graal, Steve Grocott, Sandra Kerr, Nancy Kerr, Giles Leaman, Helen MacGregor, Janet Russell, Leon Rosselson, Debbie Sanders, Kaye Umansky, Rick Wilson, Tom Wright, and guest vocalists, Elise Albrektsen (*Norway walk* contributor and Norwegian vocalist) and Jack (*Hey, Nanna, what you doin?*);

~ illustrator, Rachel Fuller, whose colours and characters warm every page, and to Joc Lucas for her graphic design, which wraps everything together;

~ Helen MacGregor and all the many readers and contributors, who checked the drafts, recalled their favourite childhood songs, taught me others, corrected my mistakes and jollied the books along: Charlie, Jake, Marco, Linda, Tim, Kevin, Eilidh, Heather, Tamar, Joyce, Rachel, Elizabeth, Jo, Polly, Sarah, Mary, Emily, Victoria, Margareta, Jody, Cina, Bethan, Abigail, Bea, Anni, Linda, Etain, Elizabeth, Charlotte, Danielle, Ali, Vicki, Maria.

WORDS AND MUSIC

• 2 *Elephants have wrinkles* by **Susan Kassirer** © Rock N Rainbow Music Publishing.

• 5 *We've grown so tall* by **Mavis de Mierre** © the estate of Mavis de Mierre.

• 8 *Ten little teddies*, 21 *Banana fingers*, 26 *Grandpa's knees*, words © 2021 by **Kaye Umansky**.

• 13 *Norway walk*, English words © 2021 **Helen MacGregor**.

• 14 *Hey, Nanna, what you doin?* © 2021 **Steve Grocott**.

17 *Umbrella Man* by **James Cavanaugh**, **Larry Stock**, **Vincent Rose** © 1924, Redwood Music Ltd, Memory Lane Music Ltd.

• 20 *Let's make a cake* by **Harriet Powell** © Harper Collins. from *Game-Songs with Prof Dogg's Troupe* ISBN 978-1-4081-9443-0 © 1983, 2001, 2013 Harper Collins Publishers Ltd.

• 24 *Mairzy doats* words and music by **Milton Drake**, **Al Hoffman** and **Jerry Livingston** © copyright 1988 EMI Miller Catalog Inc. EMI United Partnership Ltd. All Rights Reserved. International Copyright Secured. Used by permission of Hal Leonard Europe Limited.

• 27 *Climbing up my grandad* © 2021 **Sandra Kerr**.

• 33 *My great gran's a dancer* © 2021 **Leon Rosselson**.

• 34 *Magic Penny* words and music by **Malvina Reynolds** © copyright 2014 MCA-Northern Music Company Inc.Universal/MCA Music Ltd. All Rights Reserved. International Copyright Secured. Used by permission of Hal Leonard Europe Limited.

• The original words to adaptations of traditional melodies of 6 *Sunday Monday*, 10 *A finger walk*, 15 *Lefty Lucy*, 28 *Hickory dickory PLOP*; the English words to 7 *Giro tondo*, 16 *Our Good Grandma*; the adaptation of the words of 9 *Hands can dance*, 18 *Gramma say no play (Caribbean)*; and the words and music of 31 *A box of clocks* are by **Sheena Roberts** © 2021 Playsongs Publications Ltd.

• *Author unknown/public domain*: 1 *You are my sunshine* (North America), 3 *Camels* (Morocco), 4 *Mousie Brown and Grandma* (UK), 11 *Moses supposes* (UK), 12 *There was a little man* (UK), 16 *Our Good Grandma* (Greece, contributed by Kevin Graal), 19 *Buy a penny ginger* (Caribbean), 22 *Eilidh bombailie* (Fife, contributed by Eilidh Graham), 23 *Dips* (Italy, Greece, Spain, India), 25 *High-chilly-wang-wang pills* (Orkney, contributed by Andrew Appleby), 29 *Achina-ee* (Ireland), 30 *The animal fair* (North America), 32 *Hey ca' through* by Robert Burns (public domain).

Musical arrangements and audio © 2021 Playsongs Publications Ltd. All audio in *Playsongs Grand Exercise* is published and distributed under licence from PRS-MCPS.

Every effort has been made to trace and acknowledge owners of copyright lyrics reprinted in this publication. If any right been omitted, the publishers offer their apologies and following written notification will rectify any print omissions on reprint.

CONTENTS

GRAND
WARM UPS AND STRETCHES

1 You are my sunshine
2 Elephants have wrinkles
3 Camels (A ram sam sam)
4 Mousie Brown and Grandma (rhyme)
5 We've grown so tall
6 Sunday Monday (I sent a letter to my love)
7 Giro giro tondo

GRAND
FINGERS AND TOES

8 Ten little teddies (rhyme)
9 Hands can dance (Oats and beans)
10 A finger walk (The drunken sailor)
11 Moses supposes (rhyme)
12 There was a little man (rhyme)
13 Norway walk (rhyme/Anitra's Dance)

GRAND
DAY'S WORK

14 Hey, Nanna, what you doin?
15 Lefty Lucy (Humpty Dumpty)
16 Our good grandma
17 Umbrella man
18 Gramma say no play
19 Buy a penny ginger
20 Let's make a cake

GRAND
BRAIN TEASERS

21 Banana fingers (rhyme)
22 Eilidh bombailie (rhyme)
23 Dips
24 Mairzy doats

GRAND
KNEE RIDERS AND CLIMBERS

25 High-chilly-wang-wang pills (rhyme)
26 Grandpa's knees (rhyme)
27 Climbing up my grandad
28 Hickory dickory PLOP (Hickory dickory dock)
29 Achina-ee (rhyme)
30 The animal fair
31 A box of clocks (song~rhyme)
32 Hey ca' through

GRAND
FINALE

33 My great gran's a dancer
34 Magic Penny

GRAND

WARM UPS AND STRETCHES

1 YOU ARE MY SUNSHINE

You are my sunshine, my only sunshine,
You make me happy when skies are grey,
You'll never know, dear,
  how much I love you,
You're the sunshine dancing
  through my day.

**YOU ARE MY
SUNSHINE**
A swaying,
babe-in-arms,
dancing ray of
sunshine for a
gentle warm up
to an energetic
day.

2 ELEPHANTS HAVE WRINKLES

ELEPHANTS
HAVE
WRINKLES

A lumbering,
limbering,
whole body
stretch from
high, waving
trunk down to
low, stomping
toes for you and
your toddler.

On 'Why',
stretch your
arms wide and
high, bringing
them back
down to your
toes on
'yi yi yi yiih'.

Sway a little baby
in your arms and
touch each part
of her body as
you sing it.

Elephants have wrinkles, wrinkles, wrinkles,
Elephants have wrinkles, wrinkles everywhere.
On their toes, (echo)
No one knows (echo)
Why yi yi yi yiih ~

Elephants have wrinkles, wrinkles, wrinkles,
Elephants have wrinkles, wrinkles everywhere.
On their knees, (echo)
On their toes, (echo)
No one knows (echo)
Why yi yi yi yiih ~

Elephants have wrinkles, wrinkles, wrinkles,
Elephants have wrinkles, wrinkles everywhere.
On their hips, (echo)
On their knees, (echo)
On their toes, (echo)
No one knows (echo)
Why yi yi yi yiih ~

Elephants have wrinkles, wrinkles, wrinkles,
Elephants have wrinkles, wrinkles everywhere.
On their ears, (echo)
On their hips, (echo)
On their knees, (echo)
On their toes, (echo)
No one knows (echo)
Why yi yi yi yiih ~

Elephants have wrinkles, wrinkles, wrinkles,
Elephants have wrinkles, wrinkles everywhere.
On their trunks, (echo)
On their ears, (echo)
On their hips, (echo)
On their knees, (echo)
On their toes, (echo)
No one knows (echo)
Why yi yi yi yiih ~

Elephants have wrinkles, wrinkles, wrinkles,
Elephants have wrinkles, wrinkles everywhere.

3 CAMELS

Br-rum pum pum, br-um pum pum,
Gudy gudy gudy gudy gudy
    rum pum pum. (repeat)
Madavi madavi,
Gudy gudy gudy gudy gudy
    rum pum pum, (repeat)
Br-um pum pum, br-um pum pum,
Gudy gudy gudy gudy gudy
    rum pum pum. (repeat)

CAMELS
Tune: A ram sam sam
Stretch your arms out wide to either side of you.
  Make fists and raise thumbs for camels.
  Amble them towards each other, stopping for a chat at 'madavi'.
  Continue on past crossing arms over your chest, and away behind your back.
  Repeat, crossing your dominant arm below this time.

MOUSIE BROWN AND GRANDMA

Tickle your fingers up and down a little baby. As baby gets bigger, try the actions in the lyric, using baby's upstretched arm for the 'candle' and your fingers for the 'mouse'.

WE'VE GROWN SO TALL

A whole body stretch for you and your toddler. Stretch up from a crouch to tippy-toes, hands above head; come back down to a crouch, wiggling your fingers for raindrops.

Lift a little baby, high above your head, then back down into a cuddle.

4 MOUSIE BROWN AND GRANDMA

Up the tall white
   candlestick
(raise one forearm)
Crept little
   Mousie Brown,
(walk fingers up forearm)
Right up to the top
(rest mouse fingertips on
candle index finger)
But he couldn't
   get down.
(shake head sadly)
So he called to his
   grandma:
(cup hands to mouth)
Grandma!_____
Grandma!_____
But Grandma
   was in town.
So he curled himself
   into a ball
And rolled himself
   back down.
(roll fists over and over)

5 WE'VE GROWN SO TALL

We've grown
   so tall,
It must be
   all the rain,
Falling
   and falling
And falling
   down again.
We've grown
   so tall,
It must be
   all the rain,
Falling
   and falling
And falling
   down again.

6 SUNDAY MONDAY

Baby's arms are long and strong
And stretch from here to Sunday.
S U N D A Y, Sunday,
They stretch from here to Sunday.

Baby's legs are longer, stronger,
Stretching clear to Monday!
M O N D A Y, Monday,
They stretch from here to Monday.

Grandad's arms and legs are strongest,
Stretching out to August!
A U G U S T, August.
They stretch right out to August!

7 GIRO GIRO TONDO

Giro giro tondo,
Quant 'e' bello il mondo,
Gira la terra,
Tutti i bimbi a terra!

Round and round we spin spin
Such a world we spin in.
Earth never stops ~
We fall over like tops.

SUNDAY MONDAY
Tune: I sent a letter

A gentle massage for a colicky baby:

first verse: gently stretch baby's arms out to the side, open close open close across her chest;

second verse: bend knees up squeezing gently in towards the tummy, in out in out;

third verse: cradle baby on your shoulder for a comforting back pat and a wrap around hug.

GIRO GIRO TONDO

Hold baby in your arms, or pair up with a toddler. Circle around ~ and plonk down with dizzy heads.

GRAND
FINGERS AND TOES

8 TEN LITTLE TEDDIES

Ten tired teddies fast asleep,
Lying in a tangled heap.

Time to end the teddies' nap!
Up, little teddies, clap, clap, clap!

Ten busy teddies danced all day,
Time to end the teddies' play.

Shall we tuck them in their beds?
Good night, little sleepy heads.

TEN LITTLE TEDDIES

Model the actions for a toddler: your fingers are the teddies, tangled together in a snoozing heap. Jump them up and clap them into action. Dance your teddy fingers, then tuck them back to sleep in your palms.

Massage a little baby's hands while the 'teddies' sleep. Hold your thumbs out for baby to grip, while you dance your fingers, then tuck baby's hands back into yours to finish.

HANDS CAN DANCE
Tune: Oats and beans and barley

You and your toddler can copy the actions in the words; hum the tune while you massage your own and a little baby's hands.

A FINGER WALK
Tune: The drunken sailor

Cradle baby, facing you on your raised knees. March your fingers up to baby's knees and fly them like gulls. Run them down to pat baby's tummy. 'Walk' back over the 'hill' to snuggle baby's feet in your hands.

Model the actions on yourself for a toddler to copy.

9 HANDS CAN DANCE

Hands can dance and hands can jive,
Hands can clap when you arrive,
Hands can play at peeka-BOO!
Hands can blow a kiss to you.

Hands can rub when hands are cold
Hands can do whatever they're told ...

Hands can swish and hands can tap,
Hands can rest and take a nap ...

10 A FINGER WALK

A finger walk, a finger walk,
We're off to take a finger walk.
A finger walk, a finger walk,
Let's take my hand for a finger walk.

Climb the hill to see the sea,
And watch the seagulls flying free.
Run down along the strand,
And pat pat pat the golden sand.
    A finger walk ...

Skip in the waves along the shore,
Till our finger feet are tired and sore,
Then home for griddle-cakes baked for tea,
A snuggle and a cuddle for you and me!

11 MOSES SUPPOSES

Moses supposes
His toeses are roses
But Moses supposes
Erroneously.

For nobody's toeses
Are posies of roses
As Moses supposes
His toeses to be!

12 THERE WAS A LITTLE MAN

There was a little man
And he had a little crumb,
And over the mountain
He did run,
With a belly full of fat,
And a big tall hat,
And a pancake stuck
to his bum, bum, bum.

13 NORWAY WALK

Gå i skogen, gå i skogen
Hogge ved, hogge ved
Fryse på foten, fryse på foten
Springe springe springe springe springe springe ~
Hjem! hjem!

Walk to the woods, walk to the woods,
Chop some logs, chop some logs,
Freezy feet, freezy feet, freezy feet,
Freezy feet, freezy feet, freezy feet,
Run run run run run run
Run run run run run run
Run run run run run ~ HOME!

MOSES SUPPOSES
Rub baby's toes in turn as you say the rhyme.

THERE WAS A LITTLE MAN
Waggle index finger, pinch a 'crumb' off baby's mouth, run fingers over baby's crown, pat tummy, pat head, pat 'bum bum bum'.

NORWAY WALK
Tune: Anitra's Dance (Grieg)
Sit baby on your knee, facing outwards. Hold an ankle in each hand. 'Walk' baby's feet on the beat; cross and recross them over each other on 'chop'; rub toes on 'freezy feet'; 'run' feet and jump baby into the air and down on 'Home!'

14 HEY, NANNA, WHAT YOU DOIN?

Hey, Nanna, what you doin?
Nanna, what you doin now?
Hey, Nanna, what you doin?
Nanna, what you doin now?
　I'm sowing the seeds,
　That's what I'm doing,
　That's what I'm doing now.
　Sowing the seeds,
　That's what I'm doing,
　Come on and I'll show
　　you how.

Hey, Nanna, what you doin ...
　I'm planting the tatties ...

Hey, Grandad, what you doin ...
　I'm pulling up the weeds ...

Hey, Nanna, what you doin ...
　I'm watering the flowers ...

Hey, Nanna, what you doin ...
　I'm whistling with the robin ...

HEY NANNA, WHAT YOU DOIN?
Grandchildren have so many questions! And grandparents know so much! Here's a song for sharing all that experience. Change the words to suit what you're doing together.

A handy engineer's word-play for remembering which way loosens and which tightens.

Sway baby on your knee ~ way out to the left on 'squeak' then a bounce on 'bop'. Slide her to the floor and playfully tug her arms. Reverse for Righty Tighty with a woosh up and a hug on 'mend'

OUR GOOD GRANDMA

A dancing, knee-bouncing, Greek song about a grandma's busy life on her farm ~ and mending Grandpa's trousers. Dance baby in your arms while a toddler or little child freestyles.

15 LEFTY LUCY

Lefty Lucy told Thingummy Bob,
This is the way you loosen the job!
A left-handed spanner ~ squeeeeeeeak
A left-handed hammer ~ bop bop
And that's a start, it's fallen apart!
(spoken) Belt and braces give it a tug!

Righty Tighty told Hoojimmy Flick,
This is the way you tighten it quick!
A right-handed spanner ~ squeeeeeeak
A right-handed hammer ~ bop bop
And that's the end of a very good mend!
(spoken) Belt and braces, give it a hug!

16 OUR GOOD GRANDMA

Η γιαγιά μας η καλή
Έχει κότες στην αυλή
Κότες και κοτόπουλα
Χήνες και χηνόπουλα   (repeat)

Our good grandma stitches and sews,
Stitches and sews mending Grandpa's clothes.
Handle whirling, bobbin whirring,
Grandma's sewing machine will mend the world. (repeat)

Η γιαγιά μας η καλή
Έχει ραπτομήχανη
Και γαζώνει και μπαλώνει
Του παππού το πάντελόνι.   (repeat)

17 UMBRELLA MAN

Toodle-luma-luma
Toodle-luma-luma
Toodle-aye-ay,
Any um-ber-rellas,
Any um-ber-rellas
To mend today?

Bring your parasol,
It may be small,
It may be big.
He repairs them all
With what you call
A thingamajig.

Pitter patter patter,
Pitter patter patter,
Here comes the rain.
Let it pitter patter,
Let it pitter patter,
Don't mind the rain.

He'll mend your umbrella
Then go on his way,
    singing
Toodle-luma-luma
Toodle-ay
Toodle-luma-luma
Toodle-ay,
Any um-ber-rellas
To mend today?

When there's a lull
And things are dull,
He sharpens knives
For all the wives
In the neighbourhood
And he's very good.

He'll darn a sock
Or set a clock,
An apple cart,
A broken heart,
He mends anything,
But he'd rather sing

Toodle-luma-luma
Toodle-luma-luma
Toodle-aye-ay,
Any um-ber-rellas,
Any um-ber-rellas
To mend today?
He'll patch up your
    troubles
Then go on his way,
    singing
Toodle-luma-luma
Toodle-ay,
Toodle-luma-luma
Toodle-ay,
Any um-ber-rellas
To mend today? (repeat)

UMBRELLA MAN

The toodling umbrella man, who fixed umbrellas, parasols and any other thing you might want mended, came into the world in 1924, but toodled most famously in the 1939 film 'These foolish things'. The BBC reran the old films and as a child, I watched them on black and white tv, on grey, wet, Sundays ~ weather for the umbrella man.

I could never get the toodles in the right order. But it doesn't matter. It's just fun to toodle along while you dance together, and the umbrella man gets on with fixing things.

18 GRAMMA SAY NO PLAY

GRAMMA SAY NO PLAY

Small children love helping and learning from the tasks you share. Make up your own verses to suit the activity.

A little baby will enjoy you moving to the song's rhythm, as you hold him in the crook of your arm and work with the other ~ or use the song as a lively knee-bouncer or dancer.

Gramma say no play
This is a work day,
Up with the bright sun,
Get all the work done.
If you will help me,
Climb up the tall tree,
Shake the papaya down.
Shake them down,
Shake them down,
Shake the papaya
down. (repeat)

Gramma say no play
This is a work day,
Up with the bright sun,
Get all the work done.
If you will help me,
Wash the potatoes,
Splosh the potatoes round.
Splosh them round ...

Gramma say no play ...
... Fill up the washing,
Watch it go round and round ...

Gramma say no play ...
... Shake out the clean clothes,
Peg them up on the line ...

19 BUY A PENNY GINGER

Buy a penny ginger,
Pung it in de mortar,
Buy a penny ginger,
Pung it in de mortar,
Doo naka doo naka dooKAY!

20 LET'S MAKE A CAKE

Let's make a cake,
Let's make a cake,
Mix in all the things that we like best,
A little bit of this, a little bit of that,
What shall we put in first?
(pause for ideas and suggestions)
And we shall mix in the flour,
Mix in the flour, stir and stir
and stir and stir and ~

Let's make a cake,
Let's make a cake,
Mix in all the things that we like best,
A little bit of this, a little bit of that,
What shall we put in next?
(agree your next ingredient)
And we shall mix in the raisins ...
... ice cream ... rainbows ... stir and stir
and stir and stir and bake!

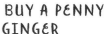

BUY A PENNY GINGER
Toddlers are great at sitting on their heels. Can you? Crouch facing your toddler, lightly holding hands and beating up and down on the 'ginger' in the 'mortar'. On 'KAY' fling your hands in the air to try and overbalance each other.

LET'S MAKE A CAKE
A mixing bowl and a wooden spoon are all you need for a pretend game of cake-making: 'and we shall mix in the pebbles/daisies/mud...' Toddlers have grand ideas.

Sing up a real cake with an older child.

GRAND

BRAIN TEASERS

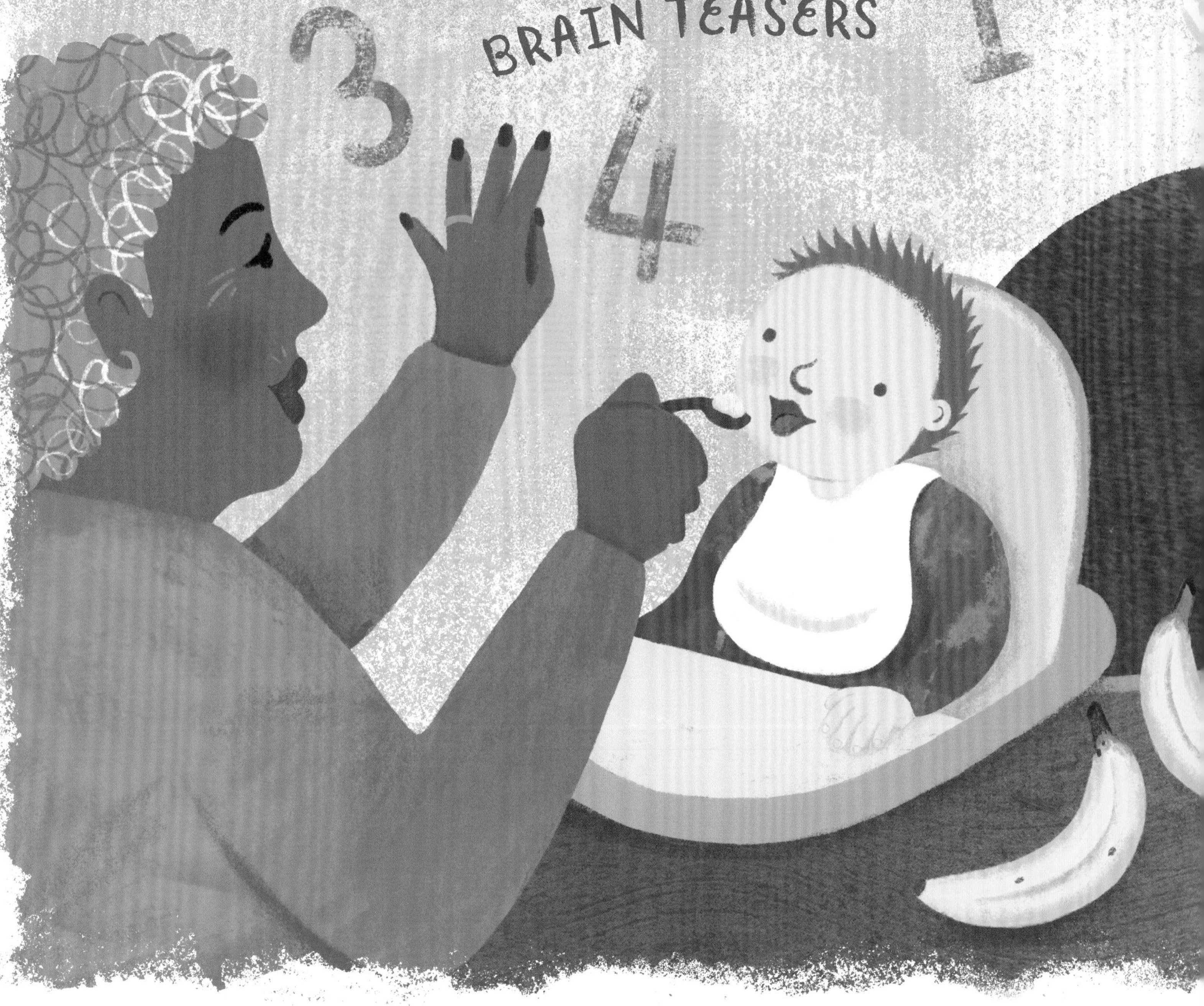

21 BANANA FINGERS

Two little monkeys
Sitting down to tea.
Who likes bananas?
You and me!
Put our bibs on
Nice and neat.
How many bananas
Did we eat?
1-2-3-4!

... How many bananas
Did we eat?
1-2-3-4-5-6!

... How many bananas
Did we eat?
1-2-3-4-5-6-7-8-9-10!

BANANA FINGERS

Count out the bananas on baby's fingers or toes. With bigger children, stop at 'eat?' and hold up your fingers for them to count.

A Fife,
children's
playground
brain teaser.
It will work for
any name once
you've got the
hang of it. Knee
bounce your
baby or toddler to
their own name,
getting faster
and faster as
you improve
your skill.

Tweak baby's
fingers or toes
on the beat of
these counting
out rhymes. With
small children, put
a raisin in each
fist and all hold
fists out to be
tapped in turn.
The raisin that's
'It' gets eaten.

These Dips are
from the UK,
Italy, Greece,
Spain and India.

22 EILIDH BOMBAILIE

Eilidh bombailie
Stickalailie fyfailie
Fyfailie stickalailie
That's how you spell
Eilidh!

23 DIPS

Dip dip dip, my blue ship
Sailing on the water
Like a cup and saucer,
You are it!

Ponte ponente ponte pi
Tappe ta Perugia
Ponte ponente ponte pi
Tappe tappe ri.

A be ba blom, tou ki the blom,
A be ba blom tou ki the blom
blim blom.

San tha pas ekeí stin vóreia Amerikí
Na deis énan eléfanta na paízei mousikí.

Un, don, din de la poli politana,
un camión que no sirve para nada.
¡Niña, ven aquí! ~ ¡Yo no quiero ir!
Un, don, din, esto sirve para ti.

Akar bakar bambay bo
Asi nabay pooray sao
Sao mein lagga dhaga
Chor nikal ke bhaga.

24 MAIRZY DOATS

I know a ditty, nutty as a fruitcake,
    goofy as a goon and silly as a loon.
Some call it pretty, others call it crazy,
    but they all sing this tune:
Mairzy doats and dozy doats and liddle lamzy divey,
A kiddley divey do, wouldn't you? Yes!
Mairzy doats and dozy doats and liddle lamzy divey,
A kiddley divey do, wouldn't you?
    If the words sound queer and funny to your ear,
    A little bit jumbled and jivey,
    Sing, 'Mares eat oats and does eat oats,
    And little lambs eat ivy.' ~ Oh!
Mairzy doats and dozy doats and liddle lamzy divey,
A kiddley divey do, wouldn't you-oo?
A kiddley divey do, wouldn't you?

MAIRZY DOATS

Grandma Pam used to sing this forties favourite to her grandchildren. Sway a little baby in your arms as you dance together to the lazy swing, and beguile a toddler or child with the words.

Can they find all the liddle lamzies hiding in the picture?

GRAND

KNEE RIDERS AND CLIMBERS

I think you need some____
I-pick-her-
umpus-
mumpus-
bumpus-
breeches-
gaiters-
high-chilly-
wang-wang
PILLS!

I think you need some more I-pick-her-umpus ...

HIGH-CHILLY-WANG-WANG PILLS

Anyone in a grump? High-chilly-wang-wang pills are the best medicine. Lift your tired toddler into your lap and slowly rock together as you chant. You may start to feel the mood improve. When it does, start moving into a knee bounce, then, on 'PILLS', lift your toddler high in the air and plop down to the floor between your knees ~ to begin again (with more energy as the pills do their work better and better).

GRANDPA'S
KNEES
A lazily
swaying warm
up to some
more hectic
fun ~ but not
without a few
bumps to the
floor.

CLIMBING UP
MY GRANDAD
Bigger babies
and toddlers
soon get the
great idea
of walking
themselves up
your body as
you hold their
hands ~ but it
will be a while
and take a bit of
practice before
they can do the
full back flip like
the bigger kids.

26 GRANDPA'S KNEES

Lovely day with a nice cool breeze,
I'm off for a ride on Grandpa's knees,
Over the hills and under the trees,
Off for a ride on Grandpa's knees ~ BUMP!

27 CLIMBING UP MY GRANDAD

I like to climb on a climbing frame,
I like to climb a tree,
And I like climbing up the stairs
When it's sleepy time for me.
I like to climb into Mummy's bed,
I like to climb a wall,
But climbing up my grandad
Is the best climb of them all!

His big strong hands
Holding mine and here I stand
On his toes, looking up at his nose,
On his shins, better leave some skin,
Now on his knobbly knees, hope he doesn't sneeze.
Balancing on his thighs, oooh what a size!
Feet on his tummy, feeling ever so funny,
Where do I go now, goodness knows!
Then it's heels over head and I'm back at his toes!
Get my breath, count to ten,
Then we can do it all over again! (repeat)
(again, again, again ...)

28 HICKORY DICKORY PLOP

Hickory dickory dock,
The mouse walked up the clock.
The clock said, 'Stop,
You've reached the top!'
Hickory dickory PLOP!

29 ACHINA-EE

Achina-ee, when I was wee
I used to sit on my granny's knee,
Her apron tore and I fell on the floor,
Achina-ee-na-ee.

30 THE ANIMAL FAIR

I went to the animal fair,
The birds and the beasts were there,
The gay baboon by the light of
    the moon
Was combing his auburn hair.
The monkey fell out of his bunk,
And slid down the elephant's trunk,
The elephant sneezed and fell
    on his knees,
And that was the end of the monkey,
    monkey, monkey monkey,
    monkey, monkey, monkey,
    monkey, monk.

HICKORY DICKORY PLOP
More grandpa ~ and grandma ~ climbing. Walk, jump, or hop your toddler up you and on the last line, 'plop' them back down ~ or when they're bigger and have got the knack, do the back flip.

ACHINA-EE
An Irish knee bouncer from a time when aprons (sometimes threadbare) were commonly worn by all who did the work of the house.

THE ANIMAL FAIR
A wild knee bouncer full of fairground bumps and slides.

A BOX OF
CLOCKS

Great
Grandfather
James was
a master
clockmaker
and we really
did have a
box of clocks
in the attic. Do
you remember
the sound of a
mantle clock,
singing its
song? Time
pieces came
in all sizes, and
they all made
sounds.

Song: rock or
sway baby on
your knee to the
slow, pendulum
swing.

Rhyme: it starts
with big, slow
knee bounces
on the
grandfather's
'tick tock'.
Double the
speed of the
bounce as
the tickers
get quicker.
(continued)

31 A BOX OF CLOCKS

When I was little, I listened to time.
Time passed with tick, and time passed with
   chime chime chime chime.
Every second of the year was a second I could hear,
When time had a song that tinged and tonged,
And time was noisy and binged and bonged bong bong ...

Clockwork folk met and bowed, how d'you do?
Time butted in with a noisy cuckoo! cuckoo! cuckoo ...
Every second of the year was a second I could hear,
When clockwork soldiers' marching feet
Were kept in step by a drummer's beat beat beat beat.

Now all is quiet, the sounds have all gone,
Time passes by, flowing silently on on on on.
Every second of the year was a second I could hear
But those old tickers are jumbled in a box,
A box in the attic that's full of clocks ~
(spoken) Shall we get them out?

A box of clocks goes TICK TOCK TICK TOCK,
A box of clocks goes tick tock tick tock
   tick tock tick tock,
A box of clocks goes ticka-ticka-ticka-ticka-
   ticka-ticka-ticka-tick ~
Cuckoo! Cuckoo! Cuckoo!
   Shake it all up!
And a box of clocks goes ticka-ticka-ticka-ticka
TICK TOCK TICK TOCK tick tock tick tock ...
Cuckoo! Cuckoo! Cuckoo!
Drop it on the floor and the springs go ~ BOING!

32 HEY CA' THROUGH

Up wi' the carls o' Dysart,
And the lads o' Buckhaven,
And the kimmers o' Largo,
And the lasses o' Leven.

Hey, ca' thro', ca' thro',
For we hae muckle ado.
Hey, ca' thro', ca' thro',
For we hae muckle ado;

We hae tales to tell,
An' we hae sangs to sing;
We hae pennies tae spend,
An' we hae pints to bring.
　　Hey, ca' thro'...

We'll live a' our days,
And them that comes behin',
Let them do the like,
An' spend the gear they win.
　　Hey, ca' thro'...

A BOX OF CLOCKS
(continued)

On 'Cuckoo' lift baby up and out into the air like a Swiss clock's cuckoo (bigger toddlers can throw their arms wide). Shake the 'box' to mix up all the ticks.

End with a slide to the floor on 'Drop' and a bouncy spring up on 'Boing!'

HEY CA' THROUGH

Robert Burns wrote this strongly rhythmic work song, which makes a grand knee-bouncer. It's a tough, workout for the one doing the bouncing, and grand fun for the one being bounced.

33 MY GREAT GRAN'S A DANCER

My great gran's a dancer, she dances for fun
By herself in the kitchen with the radio on.
Her feet go tap tapping when they hear a tune,
Then she'll dance to the sun
    and she'll dance to the moon.

My great gran's got wrinkles, her hair has gone grey
And she sometimes forgets what she's going to say,
But when she starts dancing with a skippety hop,
She whirls and she swirls and she twirls like a top.

My great gran is 80 and I'm only three
And I like it best when she dances with me.
She takes both of my hands and she teaches me how
To step this way and that way and then take a bow.

We laugh and we clap cos we're having such fun,
As we dance to the moon and we dance to the sun.
She says when she's dancing she still feels eighteen ~
My great gran's the greatest great gran ever seen.

MY GREAT
GRAN'S A
DANCER
Here's to the joy
of moving to the
tap of a tune, no
matter whether
you're three
years old or 80.

34 MAGIC PENNY

Love is something if you give it away,
Give it away, give it away.
Love is something if you give it away,
You end up having more.
It's just like a magic penny,
Hold it tight and you won't have any.
Lend it, spend it, and you'll have so many
They'll roll all over the floor. For ~

Love is something if you give it away,
Give it away, give it away.
Love is something if you give it away,
You end up having more.
Money's dandy and we like to use it,
But love is better if you don't refuse it.
It's a treasure and you'll never lose it
Unless you lock up your door. For ~

Love is something if you give it away,
Give it away, give it away.
Love is something if you give it away,
You end up having more.
So let's go dancing to the break of day
And if there's a piper, we can pay,
For love is something if you give it away,
You end up having more. For ~
Love is something if you give it away ...

MAGIC PENNY
Rock or dance a baby or toddler in your arms for a soothing wind down from an energetic day.